Might goes hand in hand with right as He-Man and the Masters of the Universe fight to make their planet safe. The greatest of their enemies is Skeletor, the Lord of Destruction, and his evil band, whose hatred for their foes is never-ending. The war goes on but who will win?

First edition

© LADYBIRD BOOKS LTD MCMLXXXIV and MATTEL INC MCMLXXXIV

The Iron Master

by John Grant
illustrated by Robin Davies

Ladybird Books Loughborough

In the Royal Palace of Eternia, all was
quiet. Suddenly the peace was broken by a cry
from the guards at the main gate. Something
was approaching. It was a peasant's ox cart.
One man led the oxen, while a second stood up
in the cart and hailed the guards. "We have a
man here badly hurt!"

The guards opened the gates and the cart rumbled into the courtyard. Hearing the commotion, King Randor hurried out. He took one look at the peasant's injuries and called for the royal doctor. And, while the doctor made his examination of the wounded man, the king asked, "Who has dared to treat one of my subjects so?"

"It was the wild men of the forest, Your Majesty," said one of the man's companions. "Lob, here, went after a strayed goat; and he had barely entered the forest when they sprang from the trees and attacked him and made off with the goat."

As the injured peasant was carried into the palace, a figure stepped out from behind a pillar. It was Prince Adam, who had seen and heard everything. "This is the work of that evil creature, Beast-Man," he said. "This is a task for He-Man."

Hurrying to an inner room of the palace, Prince Adam took out the Power Blade, the great sword forged for him by the Sorceress. He held it high and cried:

"BY THE POWER OF GRAYSKULL!"

Instantly, Prince Adam was transformed into He-Man, mightiest man in the Universe.

On the edge of the forest, He-Man stooped to examine the ground for tracks. As he did so a noose of stout vines dropped round his shoulders and pinned his arms to his sides. The Power Blade flew from his hand and stuck quivering in the ground. With a roar, the Beast-People, led by their leader Beast-Man, rushed from the trees. Beast-Man seized the sword...and next moment was screaming in agony as the hilt burned like fire in his hand.

Beast-Man dropped the sword and clutched his hand. And with his mighty strength, He-Man burst the vine holding him and sprang at the startled Beast-People. He picked up the sword and swung the Power Blade in a dazzling arc.

The Beast-People ran for the safety of the forest while He-Man stood over their leader.

"You fool," said He-Man. "Did you not know that only those who have no evil in them may handle the Sword of Power without hurt? Has your lord, Skeletor, not warned you and your

kind that even he, Lord of Destruction, may not
lay a finger on the sword because of the power
given it by the Sorceress in the hidden depths of
Castle Grayskull? Go to him now. Tell him what
happens to those who seek to harm the simple
peasants of Eternia."

From his lair in Snake Mountain, Skeletor
watched with anger as Beast-Man scuttled away
into the forest, helped on his way by a bolt of
energy from the Power Blade.

"That accursed Sword of Power," raged Skeletor. "Even I, Lord of Destruction, dare not touch it. But I wonder if a hand which is not of flesh and blood could grasp it without hurt?"

Deep in their underground workshops Skeletor's slaves, the Skelcons, prepared to construct a new weapon for their dreaded master. First they dug deep into the roots of the mountain for the iron which lay buried there. Then they tapped the fiery lava of Snake Mountain's volcanic peak to smelt the iron ore. Day and night they laboured with the raw metal until Skeletor stood before the finished work. The Skelcons trembled before Skeletor until he gave a mighty roar of satisfaction. "Behold a new Master of the Universe! An Iron Master who feels no pain! An Iron Master who can win the Sword of Power and use it in my service against He-Man and his like! Now to teach my new slave his duties!"

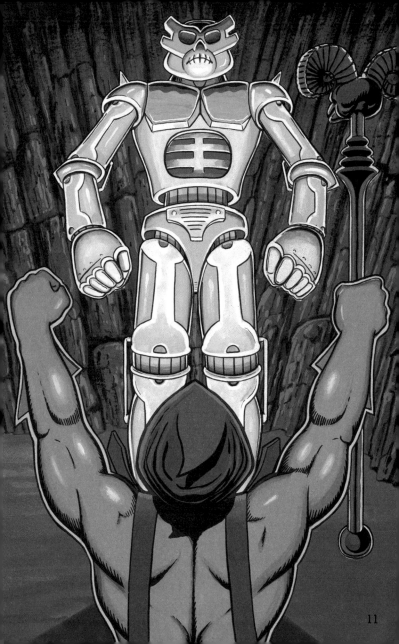

The Iron Master stood twice as tall as Skeletor
himself, who had to step back and crane
his neck to look upwards to the iron head.
Stretching out his ram-headed Havoc Staff,
Skeletor sent a charge of energy into the
mechanical brain of the robot. Slowly the eyes
began to glow. Pistons, cranks and wheels began
to move. And, with a clank of machinery and
the hiss of steam, the Iron Master raised one
iron arm in salute to its master.

Skeletor's eyes glowed as brightly as the
robot's as he sent a stream of thought energy
through the Havoc Staff.

"You have one task. Seek out and take the Sword of Power. When you have done that you will be my right hand in my war with the rulers of Eternia."

With more clanking and hissing the Iron Master strode out of the cavern in search of He-Man and the Sword of Power.

Within a few days King Randor began to hear strange reports from his subjects. A shepherd told of giant footprints in the turf of the hillside. A traveller's horse had been startled by a glimpse of a giant figure above the trees. And several peasants arrived at the palace at nightfall. They said that a huge pair of red eyes had watched their every move from the top of a hill.

At the end of a week a farmer and his family fled for refuge to the palace. A great man-shaped monster had come out of the night. With blazing eyes and a clanking of machinery it had trampled their house to pieces. They had barely escaped with their lives.

When Prince Adam heard the farmer's story he knew it was no fanciful rumour. It was the work of Skeletor. It was time for the Masters of the Universe to take a hand.

Calling on his pet Eternian tiger Cringer, Prince Adam rushed to his private apartments. Then he took up his sword and cried:

"BY THE POWER OF GRAYSKULL!"

Instantly he was transformed into He-Man, while Cringer became Battle-Cat, armoured and ready for battle.

Following the directions given by the farmer, He-Man had no difficulty in finding the scene of destruction. Huge footprints were sunk deep in the soil. They made a track right across the ruins of the farm house and through the surrounding fields and woods.

Some country people came out of hiding and told He-Man that the iron man had gone from the neighbourhood, but they feared its return.

"This is no work for one person," said He-Man to himself. And he sent out a tele-summons for Teela, Stratos and Ram-Man to meet him at Castle Grayskull to make plans for the destruction of the iron monster.

17

The red sun of Eternia was setting as He-Man leapt astride Battle-Cat and set off for Castle Grayskull. The mighty animal covered the ground in great bounds and had covered more than half the distance when He-Man halted it. He had an uneasy feeling that something was wrong. He dismounted and looked all around in the gathering darkness. There was nothing to be seen or heard. He-Man was preparing to mount again when Battle-Cat growled deep in his throat. His tail twitched and the hair stood up on his back. He had sensed something that not

even He-Man's super powers had detected.
The big cat turned and looked back the way
they had come. He-Man followed his gaze.

Something moved against the distant red
sunset. It was a giant, man-shaped figure,
striding at great speed towards He-Man.
Leaping once more on to Battle-Cat, He-Man
urged him to his utmost speed, while the
clanking thing behind him drew steadily closer.

Battle-Cat was swift, but even he was no
match for the giant strides of Skeletor's
mechanical iron monster. Through field and
forest, over rocks and rivers, Battle-Cat flew like
the wind. But, behind, the clank of machinery
and the hiss of steam grew louder and louder.
He-Man looked back over his shoulder, and in
the light of the rising moon he could now see
clearly every detail of the thing.

Soon, the ground below Battle-Cat's feet
began to shake with the heavy foot-falls of the
robot. The red light from its eyes bathed
He-Man and Battle-Cat and sparkled on the
blade of the Sword of Power.

Not a moment too soon, the turrets and battlements of Castle Grayskull came in sight.

Between He-Man and the castle lay the River of Doom. As he drew near the bank He-Man had an idea that might just gain him precious moments. He urged Battle-Cat forward and the great animal leapt over the bank. At the water's edge however they swung to the left and raced upstream under cover of the high bank. Baffled, the iron man stopped at the river. There was no sign of He-Man on the far side. Then the mechanical senses of the robot picked up the new trail. But by then, He-Man had crossed the river and the castle lay just ahead.

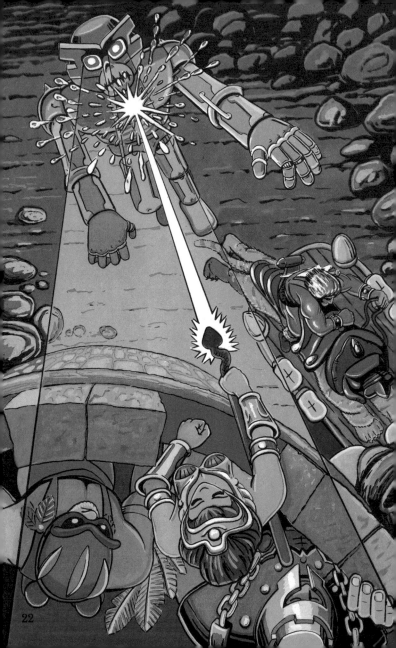

On the ramparts of Castle Grayskull Teela, Stratos and Ram-Man watched as Battle-Cat raced for the gate. Teela pressed the controls and the jaw-bridge swung open. With He-Man stretched out over his neck, Battle-Cat made a final spurt.

At the sight of the figures on the battlements the iron man stopped. It swung its head from side to side. Its red eyes flared out in a fiery glow, lighting the castle as brightly as daylight.

Teela raised her power sceptre and sent a powerful blast towards the monster. Sparks and molten metal flew from its iron body. Again and again the warrior goddess fired her weapon. The iron man seemed quite uninjured, and after a moment came after He-Man once more. But the delay had been enough. With a mighty bound Battle-Cat crossed the jaw-bridge and gained the safety of the castle. Another flick of the controls and the bridge crashed shut a moment before the robot reached the walls.

At the foot of the ramparts Skeletor's iron monster beat its metal fists on the stone. With iron fingers it tried to pull pieces from the wall itself.

Above, the Masters of the Universe watched. Again Teela sent bolt after bolt of energy at the creature. The iron body was scorched and melted where they hit, but they did no serious damage. He-Man raced along the top of the wall. He thought that he might be able to hit a vital spot from a new angle. And as he ran, the monster turned to follow him. The others watched in amazement. "It's only He-Man it's after!" cried Stratos.

He-Man drew his Sword of Power, and the iron robot lunged upwards, reaching for the sword with clutching hands.

"It's the sword!" cried He-Man. "Skeletor has fashioned this evil thing to steal the Sword of Power!"

He-Man brandished the sword above his head.
The robot became frantic in its efforts to seize
the shining blade. But, tall as it was, the castle
walls placed He-Man and his weapon
out of reach.

While He-Man used his sword to lure the iron
man, the others tried to find some spot on its
iron body where their energy weapons might
inflict serious damage. But it still stood
clutching vainly up at He-Man, ignoring the
crackling energy poured out at it.

He-Man shouted, "Cease firing! You're
wasting power on this thing. We must find
another way to destroy it...we can do nothing
while we are cooped up within the castle walls.
We have more chance if we can lure it away
and attack it in the open."

He-Man held out his sword. "Take it, Stratos," he said. "You are fighting for the side of good, and the Sword of Power will not harm you. If Skeletor's iron monster is really only after the sword, then it will follow wherever it goes."

Stratos took the sword and soared into the air. Immediately the iron man turned and reached out towards him. Stratos swooped down close above the monster's head, banking away as it

made a grab in his direction. Round and round
flew Stratos. Round and round after him turned
the robot. And all the time it was getting
farther and farther from the walls of the castle.

The thing was almost lost to view in the
darkness when He-Man said, "Now is our
chance." And he pressed the controls of the
jaw-bridge.

   With a crash the jaw-bridge swung open.
Teela sprang to the saddle of her horse and with
her power sceptre held high, clattered under the
archway and out of the castle. Behind her,
He-Man and Ram-Man followed in the
Battle-Ram.

   Soon they could see the metal creature against
the night sky. Its red eyes burned with rage as it
tried again and again to snatch the sword from
Stratos. But the Lord of the Air was too agile.

And now it sensed danger from behind. It
swung round as Teela reined in her horse and
He-Man halted the Battle-Ram close beside her.
"What do we do now?" she said.

Before He-Man could reply, Ram-Man said,
"Brute strength!" And he launched himself
forward. With an echoing "CLANG!"
Ram-Man hit the monster in its
iron midriff...and bounced back,
leaving it unharmed.

As Ram-Man picked himself up, Teela said,
"I thought I felt rain." Black storm clouds were
moving swiftly across the sky. The stars
disappeared one by one. Distant thunder
rumbled and lightning flickered.

"I have an idea," cried Teela. "Keep the
robot confused, and lead it towards the hills."

Now the Masters of the Universe began a
dangerous game. Stratos swooped down, and the

iron man made to follow him. Stratos passed the
sword to Teela, who galloped in a circle. Then,
as the monster made after her, she threw the
sword to He-Man in her turn.

Soon, they were close to the hills. The storm
was right overhead as the iron man reached the
base of a rocky peak. Stratos caught the sword
from He-Man and spiralled upwards as the rain
fell and the thunder crashed.

Circling just beyond the grasp of the iron hands, Stratos led the robot on to the lower slopes of the peak. The robot never took its red eyes from the Lord of the Air and the Sword of Power. It dragged itself over rocks and up steep slopes. The lightning flashed closer by the minute, reflecting on the iron body. The rain fell in sheets and hissed on the hot machinery. And all the time the iron monster drew nearer to the summit.

In his lair in Snake Mountain, Skeletor watched on his video-scan. This was not going as he had planned it.

"Those fools think that they can outwit my creature with their childish games," he cried.

As he watched, the Iron Master reached the top. Stratos soared upwards to safety above the thunder clouds as the robot again reached up towards the sword.

From the foot of the peak He-Man, Teela and Ram-Man watched the robot. It stood, clear against the glare of the lightning, its arms reaching up. Through an occasional gap in the thunder clouds the Masters of the Universe caught a glimpse of Stratos. The lightning came nearer. Would the plan work?

Stratos looked down. He tried to see if the monster was still on the peak. He thought he

could make out the gleam of the red eyes
through the cloud. To get a better look he
swooped downwards and banked very sharply.
As he banked, the heavy sword slipped from his
grasp. Stratos watched in dismay as it
disappeared into the darkness, too fast for him
to catch it.

With a ringing crash the Sword of Power hit
the rocks in a shower of sparks.

Skeletor watched as the iron man stooped and picked up the sword.

"At last," cried the Lord of Destruction in triumph. "The Power of the Sword is mine! All mine! I shall rule Planet Eternia with a rod of iron when my Iron Master brings the sword to me." He turned again to the video-scan. The robot still stood gripping the sword in one iron hand. Skeletor pressed the remote controls. "Obey me!" he screamed in rage. "I am your master! OBEY!"

But, instead of turning towards Snake Mountain, the iron man held the sword above his head in salute! From his metal lips came a roar of triumph.

Then, he turned to descend. But...too late! A bolt of lightning hit the tip of the upraised sword in a blaze of blue fire!

Again and again the lightning smote the iron monster. The Masters of the Universe watched in horror as the man-like machine slowly melted and crumbled. The Sword of Power was lost to view amid the smoke and fumes as the molten metal bubbled and hissed across the rocks and ran back into the earth of Eternia. Soon, there was nothing to be seen but a steaming mound of slag and cinder.

In his lair, Skeletor watched the end of his
Iron Master. His plan to seize He-Man's sword
had come to nothing. Then he laughed a
terrible laugh. "My creature is lost," he cried.
"But so is the sword. Without it those feeble
creatures from Castle Grayskull are at my
mercy. They will shortly feel the power of
Skeletor, Lord of Destruction. Nothing can stop
me now!"

On the stormy hillside, He-Man, Teela and
Ram-Man stared at the scorched rocks. Was the
Sword of Power truly destroyed? Was this the
end for the Masters of the Universe?

The storm clouds slowly passed over. The moon shone brightly on the wet rock. High above the peak Stratos circled. He saw the glowing remains of Skeletor's robot. And he saw something else. Something which gleamed cold and deadly in the moonlight. It was the sword. The power of good placed in it by the Sorceress had overcome the evil power of the iron monster. Stratos swooped down. The sword, untouched by fire or lightning, lay on top of the cinders.

At Stratos' shout, He-Man and the others
hurried to the summit of the peak.

He-Man picked up the sword. "Take heed,
Skeletor," he cried in ringing tones. "The power
of good is proof against all your evil plans, as
the Sword of Power is proof against the fire and
the lightning."